Fred Stays with Me!

by Nancy Coffelt ⌁ Illustrated by Tricia Tusa

LITTLE, BROWN AND COMPANY

New York ⌁ Boston

Sometimes I live with my mom.

Sometimes I live with my dad.

My dog, Fred, stays with me.

I still go to the same school. I still have the same friends.

But in one of my rooms I have a bunk bed,

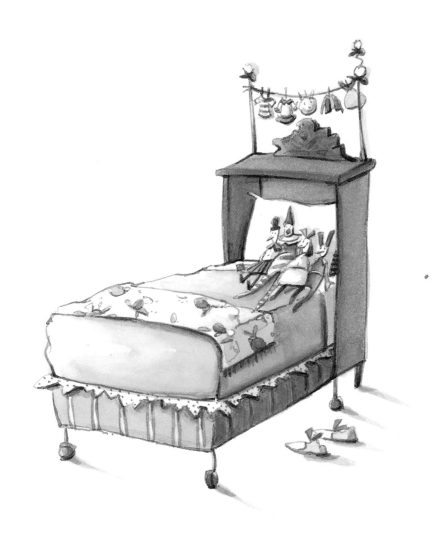

and in my other room I have a regular one.

Fred sleeps on the floor.

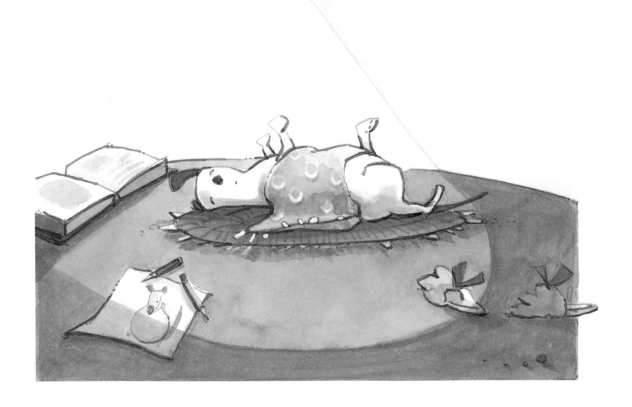

When my mom and I have pizza,
or when my dad and I eat peanut butter sandwiches,
Fred waits for crumbs.

At my mom's, Fred barks at the poodle next door.

At my dad's, Fred steals socks.

But Fred always has time to play.

My mom is tired of all the barking.

"What am I going to do with this dog?" she says.

My dad is tired of searching for socks.

"What am I going to do with Fred?" he says.

Sometimes my mom drives us to the park.
On other days my dad takes us to the lake.
Fred likes to ride in the car.

Fred shakes park mud all over the seats of my mom's car.

"What am I going to do with this dog?" my mom says.

Fred shakes lake water all over the seat of my dad's pants.

My dad says, "What am I going to do with Fred?"

Fred is my friend. We walk together. We talk together.

When I'm happy, Fred is, too. And when I'm sad, Fred is there.

But now there's trouble.

My mom is mad.
The neighbor's poodle barks at Fred all the time.

My dad is mad.
Fred has eaten all his socks.

"Fred can't stay with me!" says my mom.

"Fred can't stay with me!" says my dad.

"Fred doesn't stay with either of you.
Fred stays with ME!"

My mom and I come up with a plan.

We help Fred make friends with the poodle next door.

My dad and I come up with a plan.

We buy Fred a new chew toy and make sure all the socks are put away.

Sometimes I live with my mom.
Sometimes I live with my dad.

But Fred stays with me.

To Ernie and all other good dogs —**N.C.**

For Bear, good dog. Sit! —T.T.

Also written by Nancy Coffelt:
Pug in a Truck

Also illustrated by Tricia Tusa:
Wing Nuts

Little, Brown and Company

Hachette Book Group USA
1271 Avenue of the Americas, New York, NY 10020
Visit our Web site at www.lb-kids.com

First Edition: June 2007

Library of Congress Cataloging-in-Publication Data

Coffelt, Nancy.
  Fred stays with me! / Nancy Coffelt ; illustrated by Tricia Tusa.—1st ed.
    p. cm.
  Summary: A child describes how she lives sometimes with her mother
and sometimes with her father, but her dog is her constant companion.
  ISBN 0-316-88269-0
  [1. Dogs—Fiction. 2. Divorce—Fiction. 3. Parenting,
Part-time—Fiction.] I. Tusa, Tricia, ill. II. Title.
PZ7.C658Fre 2006
[E]—dc22

2005007973

10 9 8 7 6 5 4 3 2 1

TWP

Printed in Singapore